D1518108

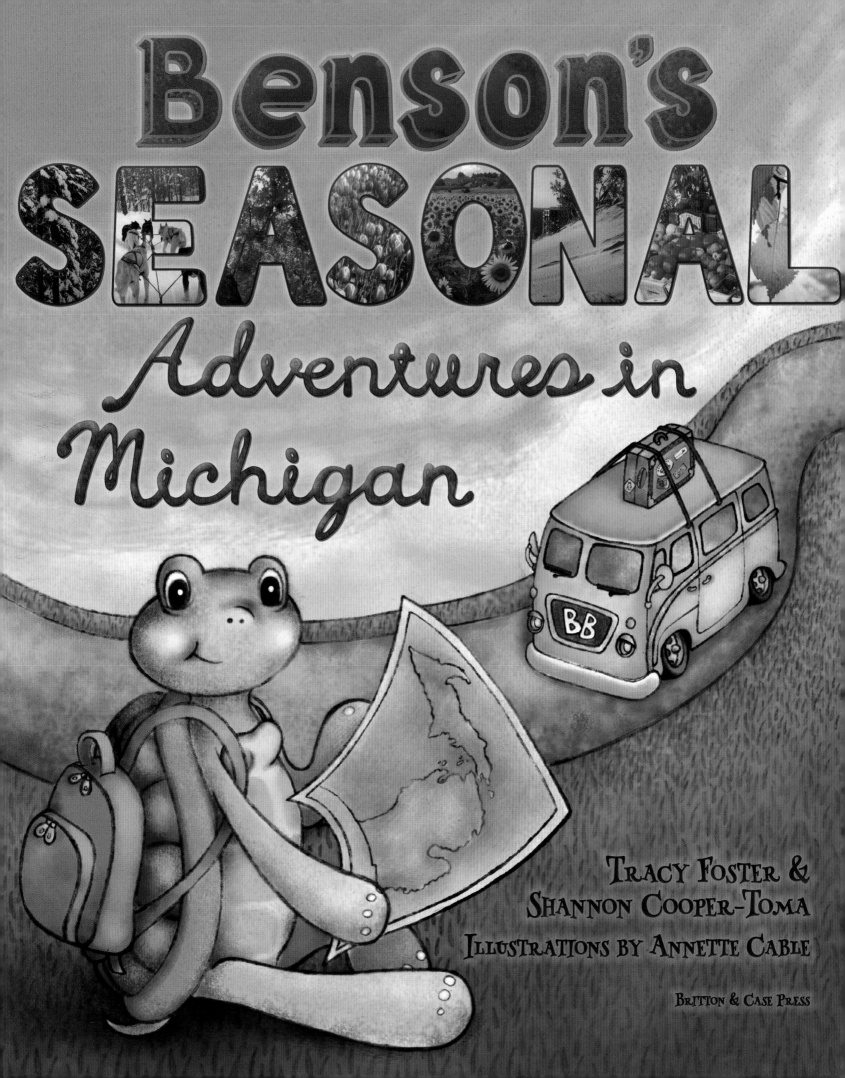

# Benson's SEASONAL

## Adventures in Michigan

TRACY FOSTER &
SHANNON COOPER-TOMA

ILLUSTRATIONS BY ANNETTE CABLE

BRITTON & CASE PRESS

©2017 TRACY FOSTER and SHANNON COOPER-TOMA

ALL RIGHTS RESERVED. No part of this publication may be reproduced, stored in a retrieval system, or transmitted in any form or by any means electronic, mechanical, photocopying, recording, or otherwise without the prior written permission of the publisher.

PUBLISHED BY

**BRITTON & CASE PRESS**

DURAND, MI


Publisher's Cataloging-in-Publication Data
Foster, Tracy.


Benson's seasonal adventures in Michigan / Tracy Foster and Shannon Cooper-Toma ;
illustrator, Annette Cable. – Durand, MI : Britton & Case Press, 2017.


p. ; cm.


Summary: Michigan, the Great Lakes state, is fun to explore in all four seasons.


ISBN13: 978-0-9980066-1-1


1. Michigan, Lake—Description and travel—Juvenile fiction.
2. Outdoor recreation—Michigan, Lake—Juvenile fiction.
I. Title. II. Cooper-Toma, Shannon. III. Cable, Annette.


GV194.M52 F67 2017

796.54209774—dc23          2017931308


*Illustrations by Annette Cable*


Printed in Malaysia by Tien Wah Press (PTE) Limited, First Printing, March 2017
21   20   19   18   17  •  5   4   3   2   1

McKenna, Coach Tom Izzo, and Hannah

We believe children should be curious, inspired, and encouraged to DREAM BIG. Coach Tom Izzo, men's head basketball coach at Michigan State University, is a true inspiration. If Coach Izzo isn't on the court, you can find him donating his time to local charities or mentoring young athletes at basketball camps. Coach Izzo believes that people who wish to be successful in life must pursue their passion, work hard, and DREAM BIG.

We would like to dedicate this book to the many inspirational leaders in our great state who inspire all children. McKenna and Coach Izzo are true heroes who continue to make a difference in the lives of others. McKenna is an ordinary 10-year-old who finds the strength to persevere and endure in spite of overwhelming obstacles. McKenna was diagnosed in June of 2016 with osteosarcoma, a very rare bone cancer. McKenna was facing the fight of her life. With God, family, and friends by her side, including her sister Hannah, she began a journey full of ups and downs and her #mckennassquad was born!

Our goal through this project is to help children understand that a world of Michigan travel adventures and opportunities awaits them and that they can make a difference by following their dreams. It is our sincere hope that *Benson's Seasonal Adventures in Michigan* will become a treasured family keepsake. May each reading inspire, encourage, and renew pride in being a citizen of the Great Lakes State.

My name is Benson, and I'm proud to live in the Great Lakes State.
Come travel with me through the seasons in Michigan...I can hardly wait!
Michigan is known for its four unique seasons of fun.
I love them all...I can't pick just one!
From dog sledding in the Upper Peninsula (What a delight!)
to sailing on Lake Huron on a warm summer's night,
Michigan is a great place to explore all year.
The van is packed; all I need is YOU and your seasonal gear.

# Winter

Let's go build a snowman!
The frosty outdoor fun
is grand.

Skiing, snowshoeing, sledding—
Michigan is a true winter
wonderland!

McMillan 302 miles
Dearborn 88.4 miles
Muskegon 107 miles
Empire 195.1 miles

# postcard

December 29

Dear Grandma and Grandpa,

Yesterday, we had the best winter adventure at Nature's Kennel in the Upper Peninsula! Over 100 dogs with wagging tails and lots of happy barks greeted us as we arrived. They were hoping to be the chosen few to take us on a dog sled ride through the beautiful woods. We helped feed the dogs and learned how to harness the dog team to the sled. I was excited to lead my own team on the trail! We ended the adventure with hot chocolate and cookies inside the cabin. I can't wait to show you our pictures!

Love,
Benson

Grandma and Grandpa Wendling

530 Miller Rd.

Newberry, MI 49868

*Nature's Kennel Sled Dog Racing and Adventures*

## DID YOU KNOW?

**Did you know mushers do not call out "Mush"? Instead, when they want the team to move, they call out "Let's go!" They also say "Gee" for the team to turn right and "Haw" when they want the team to turn left.**

## PEANUT BUTTER BALLS

**1 1/2 cups peanut butter**

**1/2 cup margarine or butter**

**1 pound powdered sugar**

**1 teaspoon vanilla**

**1 1/2 cups chocolate chips**

**Shortening**

*Mix peanut butter, margarine or butter, powdered sugar, and vanilla in bowl. Shape into 1" balls and refrigerate. Melt chocolate with a bit of shortening in a double boiler. Insert toothpick into refrigerated balls and dip into chocolate. Cool on wax paper and store in refrigerator or freezer.*

**BENSON'S MUSHER CHALLENGE:**
Drive your own dog team or take a ride in the sled. Be sure to post a picture or video of your experience on my website at www.BensonsAdventures.com as you enjoy a dog sledding adventure.

# postcard

January 9

Dear Addison, Cayden, Morgan, and Rohan,

I spent the day sledding on the biggest hill—the Dune Climb at the Sleeping Bear Dunes National Lakeshore! Most people think the dunes are only open during the summer, but did you know that winter is also a great time to climb them? I felt like I was flying as my sled raced to the bottom. Let's plan a visit there soon. You have to experience this one-of-a-kind Michigan adventure!

Your cousin,

Benson

The Reiber Family

805 Franklin St.

Eagle River, MI 49950

*Sleeping Bear Dunes National Lakeshore*

## DID YOU KNOW?

**Did you know that you will find the world's largest collection of freshwater sand dunes along the shores of the Great Lakes?**

### BENSON'S SLEDDING CHALLENGE:

Have an outdoor adventure sledding down the Dune Climb at Sleeping Bear Dunes National Lakeshore. Post a picture of your winter fun on my website.

# postcard

January 28

Dear Cole, Reid, and Evan,

From snowshoeing along Lake Michigan to racing down a luge track, the Muskegon Winter Sports Complex is a great way to explore winter sports in Michigan! My sister's favorite activity was ice skating along the lit trail into the beautiful woods. After our adventures, we had delicious hot soup in the lodge. Michigan has so many fun things to do in every season.

See you soon,

Benson

The Birmingham Family

201 E. Washington Ave.

Chesaning, MI 48616

## DID YOU KNOW?

Did you know the snurfer was invented in Muskegon? Did you know it was the inspiration for the modern snowboard?

**Muskegon Winter Sports Complex**

**BENSON'S LUGE CHALLENGE:**

Enjoy going down a luge track, ice skating, cross-country skiing, sledding, or snowshoeing along Lake Michigan. Post a picture of your favorite outdoor activity at the Muskegon Winter Sports Complex on my website.

February 6

Dear Claire and Ava,

This weekend, my family and I stepped back in time and explored The Henry Ford. We learned more about the history of our great country and some of its amazing inventors and leaders. We saw the real presidential vehicles of John F. Kennedy and Ronald Reagan, the famous Rosa Parks bus, and Abraham Lincoln's chair from the Ford Theatre. We also had fun inventing in the hands-on labs. This national historic landmark not only brought history to life, but it also taught me never to give up on my dreams.

Missing you,

Benson

# postcard

MICHIGAN

MICHIGAN
GREAT LAKES STATE

43 USA

Claire and Ava Martin

1009 Zimmer Ln.

Byron, MI 48418

## DID YOU KNOW?

Did you know The Henry Ford is our nation's largest indoor/outdoor history complex?

**The Henry Ford**

CLEVELAND AVE

Equal Rights

**BENSON'S INNOVATOR CHALLENGE:**
Touch history and post a picture of your favorite exhibit at The Henry Ford on my website.

7

Spring

Holland 91.2 miles

Mackinac Island 236.6 miles

Detroit 898 miles

With Holland tulips blooming in spring,
what new outdoor adventures
will Michigan bring?
Hiking, biking, baseball, and such—
I love Michigan springtime so much!

# postcard

MICHIGAN
43 USA

April 2

Dear Uncle Dan,

Mom and Dad purchased tickets in the second deck to watch the Detroit Tigers! It was my first visit to Comerica Park, so they gave me a special "First Game" certificate. We had our picture taken with Paws, too! It was "Kids Day," so after the game, I was able to run the bases. It was an amazing experience. I hope I can visit again this summer.

Your buddy,

Benson

Dan Sanford

1976 Liberty St.

Saint Joseph, MI 49085

*Comerica Park*

**BENSON'S BASEBALL CHALLENGE:**
Have fun running the bases after the game on "Kids Days." Post a picture or video on my website of your sporting adventure.

## DID YOU KNOW?
*Did you know an average of 30,000 hot dogs are sold at each baseball game in Detroit? What is your favorite baseball treat?*

# postcard

MICHIGAN
GREAT LAKES STATE

MICHIGAN

April 24

Dear James and Hazel,

Guess what! I went snowmobiling, biking, fishing, and kayaking all in one day. Do you know what's even more unbelievable? I did it all in the big city! The Outdoor Adventure Center has everything you love about the outdoors in downtown Detroit. Let's visit together soon!

Love,

Benson

James and Hazel Kelley

416 Oak Grove Dr.

Ishpeming, MI 49849

## TRAIL MIX

- 1 cup toasted oat cereal
- 1 cup cheese crackers
- 1 cup cherry-flavored dried cranberries
- 1 cup cashews
- 1 cup miniature chocolate chips or chocolate candies
- 1 cup peanut butter or butterscotch chips
- 1 cup miniature pretzel twists

*Throw everything together in a sealed container and mix. Store in a cool, dry area.*

## DID YOU KNOW?

Did you know there are over 150 different species of fish in Michigan?

*Outdoor Adventure Center*

## BENSON'S CITIZEN SCIENTIST CHALLENGE:

Become a citizen scientist! Find out what you can do as a citizen to preserve Michigan's natural resources. Share your pledge on my website.

# postcard

May 7

Dear Mason and Bella,

It was a perfect bright spring morning on Mackinac Island, so we decided to rent bicycles from Ryba's Bicycle Rentals. The lilacs were in bloom. We stopped often to take pictures and smell the beautiful purple flowers. We also dipped our toes in Lake Huron...brrr! The water was still very cold! We hope to return to the island this summer. Do you think you can join us?

Love,

Benson

Mason and Bella Cunningham

201 S. Line St.

Crystal Falls, MI 49920

Mackinac Island

## DID YOU KNOW?

Did you know the apple blossom is our state flower? It's a beautiful sight and a sure sign of spring in Michigan!

**BENSON'S CYCLIST CHALLENGE:**
While riding your bike around Mackinac Island, be sure to visit Skull Cave, Arch Rock, and Fort Mackinac. Post your pictures on my website.

# postcard

June 12

Dear Connor, Tye, and Josh,

Who knew you could travel to Holland, Michigan, to learn about the Netherlands? When we arrived, we were fitted for our very own wooden shoes, and we wore them throughout our tour of the village. During our visit, the guides taught us what life was like in the 1700s. We learned a fun Dutch dance, how to make a special Dutch cookie, and toured the old Dutch schoolhouse. It was fun exploring a new country and its traditions right here in Michigan.

Sincerely,

Benson

MICHIGAN
43 USA

MICHIGAN
GREAT LAKES STATE

The Siddock Family

685 Cherry Ln.

Hillsdale, MI 49242

Nelis' Dutch Village

## DID YOU KNOW?

**Did you know the wind turbines we see throughout Michigan are highly modernized versions of the Dutch windmill?**

**BENSON'S DUTCH CHALLENGE:**
Stop by the Old Dutch Schoolhouse to learn a few Dutch words and explore what school was like long ago.

# Summer

Swimming, boating, fishing—
let's play in the bright, warm sun.
Building sandcastles on the beach,
Michigan's the place for summer fun!

**DID YOU KNOW?**

Did you know that when lightning hits the sand, it melts and fuses the grains together into a fulgurite? Fulgurites are rare and fragile but can be found on Michigan sand dunes!

# postcard

MICHIGAN

MICHIGAN 49 USA

GREAT LAKES STATE

June 26

Dear Mom and Dad,

Thank you for letting me travel with Aunt Sue to the Silver Lake Sand Dunes. We had so much fun with our travel guide from Mac Wood's Dune Rides. Not only was he funny, but he also taught us a lot about this Michigan natural wonder. Zooming up and down the big dunes and fishtailing around the corners was a thrill! We have to take a family trip soon. You will have so much fun!

Love,
Benson

Don and Jeanne Smith

1358 Niver Rd.

Ontonagon, MI 49953

*Mac Wood's Dune Rides*

**BENSON'S DUNE SCOOTER CHALLENGE:** Search for a fulgurite during your dune ride. If you find one, be sure to post a picture of it on my website.

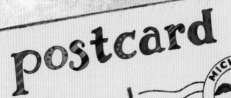

# postcard

July 3

Dear Tom,

Today I visited the Iron Mountain Iron Mine and learned about mining life in the 1800s. We traveled 2,600 feet down into the cold damp cave to view the drifts and stopes. I'm so glad they provided us with rain jackets and hard hats! We saw interesting rock and ore formations that are millions of years old. I felt like a real geologist!

Your friend,

Benson

Tom Daugherty

599 Wiltshire Dr.

Leland, MI 49654

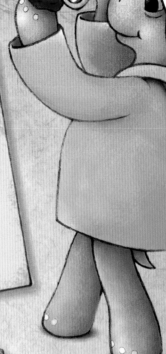

*Iron Mountain Iron Mine*

## DID YOU KNOW?

Did you know the temperature in the iron mine stays approximately 43 degrees Fahrenheit all year long?

## FRESH STRAWBERRY POPSICLES

- 1 cup fresh strawberries
- 1 cup milk
- 1/2 cup plain or vanilla Greek yogurt
- 1 tablespoon maple syrup
- 3/4 tablespoon lemon juice

*Combine strawberries, milk, yogurt, maple syrup, and lemon juice in a blender. Blend until smooth and pour into popsicle molds. Freeze for 20–30 minutes. To serve, let the popsicle molds sit at room temperature for about 5 minutes before removing the popsicles.*

## BENSON'S MINER CHALLENGE:

Enjoy a pasty, a true Upper Peninsula meal! Take a picture and tell me what you loved most about this delicious and traditional food on my website.

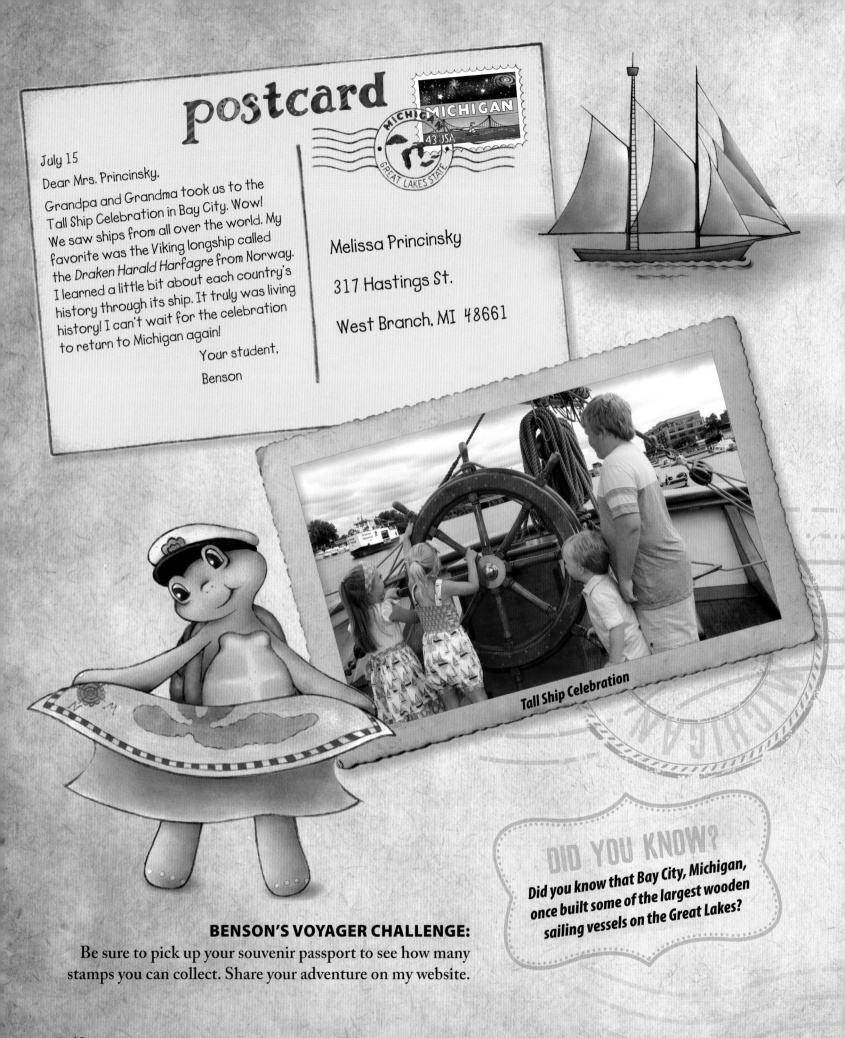

# postcard

July 15

Dear Mrs. Princinsky,

Grandpa and Grandma took us to the Tall Ship Celebration in Bay City. Wow! We saw ships from all over the world. My favorite was the Viking longship called the *Draken Harald Harfagre* from Norway. I learned a little bit about each country's history through its ship. It truly was living history! I can't wait for the celebration to return to Michigan again!

Your student,

Benson

Melissa Princinsky

317 Hastings St.

West Branch, MI  48661

**Tall Ship Celebration**

**BENSON'S VOYAGER CHALLENGE:**
Be sure to pick up your souvenir passport to see how many stamps you can collect. Share your adventure on my website.

**DID YOU KNOW?**
Did you know that Bay City, Michigan, once built some of the largest wooden sailing vessels on the Great Lakes?

# postcard

August 10

Dear Uncle Sean,

Yesterday, my family and I took a night sky cruise on Shepler's Ferry under a beautiful full moon. As the ferry cruised under the Mackinac Bridge, we learned more about the cycles of the moon and had fun listening to folklore, songs, and our captain's stories. I couldn't believe how many more stars we could see away from the city. Visit soon so we can search for constellations together.

Love,

Benson

Sean McLaughlin

485 E. McArthur St.

Mount Pleasant, MI 48858

**Shepler's Mackinac Island Ferry**

## DID YOU KNOW?

**Did you know Michigan is also a great spot to see the Aurora Borealis, or the northern lights?**

## BENSON'S ASTRONOMER CHALLENGE:

Use the night sky map given to you as you board the boat and see how many constellations you can find in the night sky. Which constellation is your favorite? Post it on my website.

# Autumn

Autumn in Michigan means...
donuts and fresh apple cider,
football games, hayrides,
and a cozy fall bonfire!

Brighton 46.4 miles
Grand Rapids 67.7 miles
Detroit 89.8 miles
Fenton 59 miles

# postcard

MICHIGAN
43 USA
MICHIGAN
GREAT LAKES STATE

September 24

Dear Blake and Marlee,

Last week, Dad took us to Ford Field. Watching the Detroit Lions play football is a great way to spend a Sunday in the fall. Dad said he is going to bring us back for a tour of Ford Field. We will get to see a locker room and stand on the field like real football players. I can't wait to run out of the tunnel!

Your friend,

Benson

Blake and Marlee Schummer

475 Lincoln St.

Rogers City, MI 49779

## DID YOU KNOW?

*Did you know many Michiganders spend the Thanksgiving holiday with their families watching Detroit Lions football? It is one of the oldest traditions in the NFL and was established by former Lion's owner G. A. Richards in 1934.*

*Ford Field*

**BENSON'S FOOTBALL CHALLENGE:**
There are many fall traditions in Michigan.
Share one of your favorite traditions on my website.

# postcard

MICHIGAN

MICHIGAN USA
GREAT LAKES STATE

October 1

Dear Uncle Rod,

My family and I spent Saturday afternoon at Spicer Orchards. What a fun-filled fall day! We enjoyed the wagon ride and walking through the corn maze, and we had fun picking out the perfect pumpkin. I am already planning how to carve it. As a special treat, Mom and Dad let us each choose a caramel apple to take home. Do you have your perfect pumpkin yet?

Love,

Benson

Rod Emmendorfer

16168 Stuart Rd.

Port Huron, MI  48060

## PUMPKIN DIP

1 15-ounce can pure pumpkin

1 5-ounce box instant vanilla pudding

1 16-ounce container whipped topping

1/2 teaspoon allspice

1/2 teaspoon nutmeg

2 teaspoons cinnamon

1/2 teaspoon ginger

*Mix all ingredients in a large bowl by hand. Chill for several hours. Serve with ginger snaps, apple slices, or graham sticks.*

*Spicer Orchards*

## DID YOU KNOW?

*Did you know the average pumpkin contains approximately 500 seeds? The number of seeds depends on the weight and size of the pumpkin.*

## BENSON'S ORCHARD CHALLENGE:

Visit a Michigan orchard. Go on a hayride, pick apples, choose a pumpkin, or find your way through a corn maze. Post your favorite thing to do at the orchard on my website.

23

# postcard

October 5

Dear GramE,

This week, my teacher took our class on a field trip to ArtPrize in Grand Rapids. We saw street performers, paintings, and unbelievable exhibits on display. I was so inspired by the unique creations that I can't wait for Ms. Cucksey's art class so I can make my very own masterpiece. Do you have a favorite artist?

Your grandson,

Benson

Edna Stephens

350 Sunset Dr.

Adrian, MI 49221

### DID YOU KNOW?

*Did you know that ArtPrize is recognized as the most attended public art event on the planet?*

**ArtPrize**

## BENSON'S ARTPRIZE CHALLENGE:

Be sure to stop by the STEAM Village to express your creativity in science, technology, engineering, art, and math. Post a picture of your innovation on my website.

# postcard

MICHIGAN
.43 USA
GREAT LAKES STATE

November 10

Dear Ellie and Anna,

Mom and I spent this beautiful fall morning horseback riding on the trails at the Brighton Recreation Riding Stable. It was so much fun riding and looking at the pretty fall leaves. Mom said she would sign me up for riding lessons soon. The next time you visit, we will go on a ride!

Missing you,

Benson

Ellie and Anna Johnson

135 Walnut Ln.

Union City, MI 49094

**Brighton Recreation Riding Stable**

**BENSON'S EQUESTRIAN CHALLENGE:**
Enjoy a horseback trail ride at Brighton Recreation Area State Park with your family. Be sure to post pictures on my website.

**DID YOU KNOW?**
Did you know Michigan has more than 200 miles of horseback riding trails? You can find the trails in state parks, recreation areas, campgrounds, and state forests.

Michigan is fun to explore in all four seasons.
I sure love it and can't wait to hear YOUR reasons!
Whether it's winter, spring, summer, or fall,
there's always a great adventure to be had by all!
As you enjoy each season in our Great Lakes State,
be sure to share your memories with me...I can hardly wait!

# About the Authors

**TRACY FOSTER**, Corunna Public Schools' 2015–2016 Teacher of the Year, has more than twenty years of experience teaching elementary and middle school children. She holds multiple degrees in education from Western Michigan University and Saginaw Valley State University. Throughout her career, she has served on various educational committees, mentored new educators, and has presented at the Michigan Reading Association Conference. She is also a member of the Michigan Reading Association and is currently an ASD Start Building Coach.

Tracy is a passionate educator who believes in empowering all students to be the best they can be and in presenting constant learning opportunities for each of them to DREAM BIG.

Tracy and her husband, Dan, are native Michiganders. They have a son, Nathan, and two daughters, Felicia and Mya. The Fosters live in Durand, Michigan, and enjoy traveling throughout the Great Lakes State. Tracy can be contacted at Tracy@BensonsAdventures.com.

**SHANNON COOPER-TOMA** is currently the building principal of an exceptional early childhood building in Corunna, Michigan. She has served as a teacher and principal in the public schools for more than seventeen years. She has received multiple degrees from Michigan State University and Saginaw Valley State University. Throughout her career, she has served on several educational committees and presented at the Bureau of Educational Research and the Michigan Reading Association conferences. Shannon is a member of the Michigan Reading Association, Association for Supervision and Curriculum Development, and Michigan Elementary and Middle School Principals Association. When asked about her career, Shannon shares, "I am passionate about empowering students to see themselves as confident readers and writers."

Shannon and her husband, Rod, reside in Owosso, Michigan, with their adorable Chihuahua named Rocko. Shannon can be contacted at Shannon@BensonsAdventures.com.

*Benson's Seasonal Adventures in Michigan* is the second book in the Benson's Adventures series. To learn more about each of the books in the series and the authors' various projects or to post pictures or videos of your adventures in Michigan, please visit www.BensonsAdventures.com.

# About the Illustrator

**ANNETTE CABLE** grew up in the country outside of Columbus, Ohio, on a farm with her four younger brothers and lots of cows. She graduated from the Columbus College of Art and Design in advertising and illustration and now calls Louisville, Kentucky, her home. She has illustrated twenty children's picture books to date, designs and illustrates for several local historical museums, and teaches children's art classes. From her drawing board and computer screen, she creates book illustrations and wall murals and designs art classrooms and community centers. Regardless of the project, her teaching philosophy encompasses creativity, community, and education.